Anything For You

and

As Long As I Live

AMY LAURENS

OTHER WORKS

Anything For You

and

As Long As I Live

INKLET #30

AMY LAURENS

Inkprint PRESS

www.inkprintpress.com

Print ISBN: 978-1-925825-29-9
eBook ISBN: 9781393713791

www.inkprintpress.com

National Library of Australia Cataloguing-in-Publication Data
Laurens, Amy 1985 –
Anything For You and As Long As I Live (Double Issue)
52 p.
ISBN: 978-1-925825-29-9
Inkprint Press, Canberra, Australia
1. Fiction—Fantasy—Dark Fantasy 2. Fiction—Short Stories

First Print Edition: March 2020
Cover image © Himanshu Gunarathna via Pixabay
Cover design © Inkprint Press
Interior art © Amy Laurens

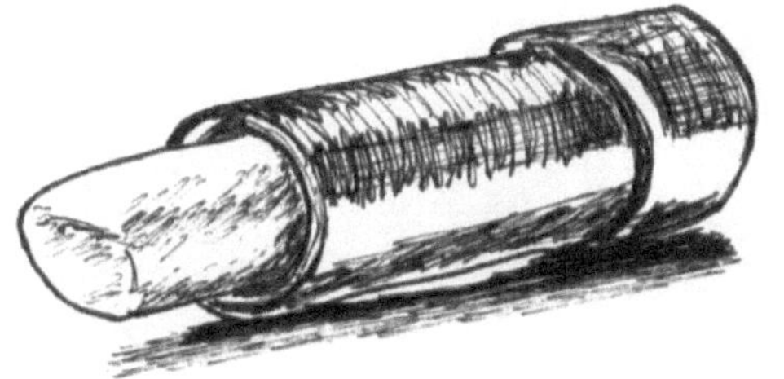

ANYTHING FOR YOU

I TURNED TO JACQUIE AND TILTED MY head under the bright lights of my closet-turned-dressing room. "What do you think?" I knew her too well to think she'd lie.

Her face fell. "Oh, honey. That colour is all wrong for you!"

My stomach sank. "What? No! I asked the woman at the counter! She did a skin test and everything!" I whirled back to the mirror and scrutinised my jawline. Sure enough, if I craned my neck up and tilted to the right, a line of orange traced my jaw from chin to earlobe.

"What am I going to do?" I turned to Jacquie in a panic. "The formal's in"—I checked the big old train station clock on the wall—"three hours and I have a hair appointment and I have to get dressed and we have to drive there, and besides all that, I'm broke!"

I buried my hands in my face and tried to pretend I wasn't sobbing over makeup. After all, children somewhere were dying of starvation. Those children probably weren't preparing simultaneously for their senior formal *and* their first date with the love of their high school life though, to be fair.

"Return it," Jacquie said. "It's the only thing you can do."

"It's opened!" I wailed. "They'll never take it back! I'm broken! The whole evening is ruined!"

Jacquie took me by the arm and marched me out my bedroom door as I waved the open tube of foundation vaguely.

"You've clearly never seen me negotiate," she promised as we climbed into the car. "Don't worry. Everything will be fine. You know I'll do anything to make this date perfect for you. It's going to be fine."

We waited as the shop assistant at the big department store's cosmetics counter served three other people ahead of us, fluorescent lights glinting off mirrors placed strategically around us, and off the silver lids of rows and rows of little pots of metallic mineral eye shadows, the caps of coloured eye pencils, and the silver signature on the sleek sides of tubes of concealers and highlighters.

Finally, it was our turn.

"How may I help you?" the perfectly-coiffed woman asked, her blond hair piled atop her head and flawless makeup smoothing her cheeks.

Jacquie pinned her with a steely stare. "We need to exchange some makeup," she said firmly, placing the foundation tube down on the glass countertop.

The woman gave it a cursory glance and plastered a false smile in place, all bright-red lips and dead, uncaring eyes. "I'm sorry, this has been opened. No returns on opened items."

Jacquie plunked our ace down on the table: the list on store letterhead detailing the makeup the previous assistant had recommended for me. "In this case," she said, "I believe you should make an exception. As you can see, the colour"—she squinted at the list—"*Sharryn* recommended for my friend here"—she gestured at me—"is all wrong."

The store woman glanced at me and I tilted my head obligingly, clearly revealing the line of orange along my jaw that we'd left in place for evidence.

She frowned. "Well. I am sorry, and you can be certain that Sharryn will be reprimanded. In cases such as this it is ordinarily possible to make an exchange, but I'm afraid you've purchased Hellfire foundation. Did you read the fine print *at all?*" she added with the scathing tone of one used to dealing with idiots on a regular basis, arching one perfect eyebrow at me.

Stomach fluttering with trepidation, I shook my head.

She handed back the list, bypassing Jacquie's outstretched hand rather pointedly, and I skimmed to the bottom of the page.

The usual disclaimers were there, indemnifying the store against skin damage, allergic reactions and so forth—and there, right at the end, in print so tiny I had to hold the paper an inch from my nose to read it, a final clause: *Purchasers agree that along with any financial exchange the store sees fit to apply, all purchases of Hellfire products shall paid for with the irredeemable giving over of the purchaser's soul.*

Purchases of Hellfire products are final, non-refundable, and non-exchangeable, except where a soul of greater value may be applied with the willing consent of the soul-owner.

What the hell?

Great.

Where was I going to get a willing soul of greater value with this short notice? My hair appointment was in less than thirty minutes.

I pressed the list to my forehead and sighed. The paper smelled vaguely of Beyonce's latest signature perfume—a fresh blend of something light and berry-like, undercut with a compli-cated tropical sort of scent—probably because Jacquie had been carrying the page around, and she'd been practically bathing in that perfume since she'd bought it last week.

Oh.

Oh.

I squinted at the clause.

"What is it?" Jacquie asked. "What's the problem?"

There was *one* option, of course... "Jacquie?" I said, voice even although my heart was hammering at my chest.

"What? Why can't you exchange it?" She peered worriedly at me, brown eyes wide.

My heart pounded. "You know how you owe me that favour?"

Her brow creased. "Well sure. But—"

"Would you be willing to do it for me now?" I said, cutting over her.

"Um, yes? I guess so. I don't know how that will help, though." She turned to the shop woman, puzzled.

The woman lifted a considering eyebrow at me.

"Well?" I said. "She's willing. Hers is of greater value, isn't it?" Of course it was; Jacquie was an angel. I, on the other hand, was self-evidently not.

The woman's other eyebrow joined the first. "Yes." She turned to Jacquie. "If you'll just come with me, Miss, I'm sure we can get this all sorted out."

"Um, okay?" Jacquie shot me a puzzled glance before following the shop assistant to a small, white door to the left of the counter that had been barely noticeable until the shop assistant had gestured at it.

I smiled and nodded encouragingly. "Thank you!" I called. "Thank you so much!"

I couldn't give up my first date with Matt. He was the love of my high school life, after all.

Jacquie would understand.

Eventually.

THE MAKING OF
ANYTHING FOR YOU

August 2015 was a good month in my life. Not outstanding in any particular way, but a good month at the end of a relatively challenging period of time. Things had finally settled after having my daughter and moving back to my home town; the house was cold but the sun often streamed in through the big windows to warm the new rug we'd bought, and the baby was sleeping through the night.

All of which is to say, I have no idea why such a wicked little story emerged at that time.

It was a Darkness and Good story, no doubt, fodder for the mostly-weekly mostly-unedited short story blog Liana Brooks and I were running at the time, and I know I'd been working through a flash fiction writing course a couple of months earlier, working on twist endings and what not.

But trading your soul for a tube of make-up? I'm afraid I have very little recollection of what led to this authorial decision, other than a vague sense of wondering just exactly how far someone might go to achieve that 'perfect look' for an important night of their life…

I mean, looking your best can be important, absolutely.

Probably shouldn't trade your best friend's soul for it though.

Just saying.

AS LONG AS I LIVE

I DIDN'T *MEAN* TO ABDUCT THE KING. Honest I didn't. I'd meant to be good, meant to keep my oath of fealty to him as long as he still drew breath. It wasn't *my* fault he'd chosen that day to be out in a paddock full of cows.

I'd snatched up the first thing I'd been able to reach, assuming it was one of nearly a hundred practically identical black beefers. Honestly, I think I was more surprised than the king was.

"How dare you!" the king blustered as I set him gently on the ground outside my lair. "What did I tell you? If you so much as *touch* another human being, I'll have you slaughtered for meat and magic!"

I ducked my head, embarrassed. "I really am sorry, your Majesty. I was aiming for the cows."

"I don't care what you were aiming for! You picked up *me*!" He straightened his tunic and glared. "I'll not kill you yet, but you will pay for this." He turned on his heel and marched away, but over his shoulder something sleek and dark and dangerous fluttered.

I shrank back, but the glittering darkness homed in. It wound me in silken folds; I shrieked as my wings shredded.

The darkness lifted. The king threw one last look over his shoulder. "You'll never fly to search for prey as long as I live, dragon. It's over. Curl up and die."

Usually, I would have done.

For a dragon, I've been pretty obedient, ever since the king took my egg from my mother and left me in my cave. But this was death by slow starvation. I wasn't *that* obedient.

As long as he lived? I could help with that.

I pounced.

He tasted pretty good, even if my wings did itch a bit as they healed.

THE MAKING OF *AS LONG AS I LIVE*

This little flash fic was a piece I wrote for a course on flash fiction writing that I was doing sometime in the middle of 2015.

With this story in particular, I was practising the idea of twist endings in flash fiction. And, being a pun-lover, English teacher, and Queen of the Dad Jokes kind of person myself, I quite liked the idea of the king accidentally signing his own death warrant through his sloppy use of language.

Precision, yo. It's important.

I tell my students frequently that, if I could, I would tattoo one word on each of their hands:

Clear.

Precise.

This is because, when students try to write in formal diction, they often mistake 'formal' for 'fancy', and end up using big words where a diminutive one would have sufficed, to paraphrase that old saying.

But clarity and precision of language have benefits far beyond the grade you're going to get on your latest English essay, obviously.

You never know. One day they might even save your life. Ha.

DOWNLOAD YOUR FREE EBOOK

When you buy a print book from Inkprint Press, we like to say THANK YOU by offering you the ebook for free!

Please head to www.inkprintpress.com/inklets/30/ and the use the coupon INKLET30 to get your copy of this Inklet in epub AND mobi today!
(Coupon will only work once.)

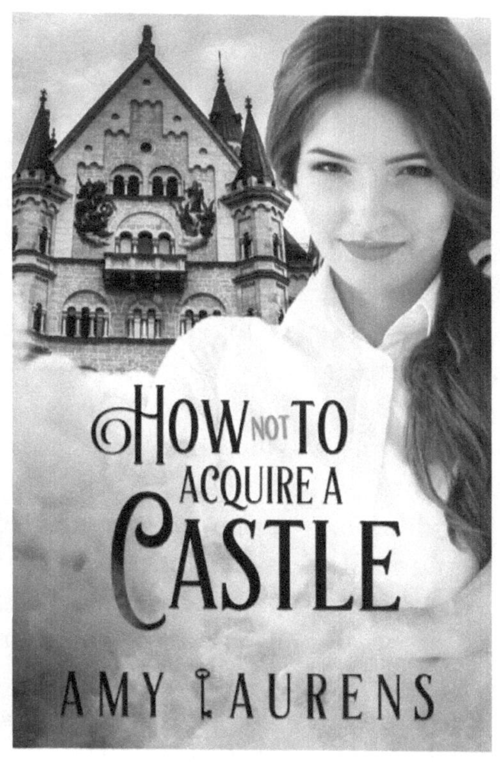

HOW NOT TO ACQUIRE A CASTLE

CHAPTER ONE

ON A HARD PLASTIC CHAIR IN THE FRONT row of the Great Hall in the world's fifth-best evil overlording academy, with its red-wooden parquetry floor that spoke of wealth and the beige, square panels of sound-boards speaking of conservatism on the walls, Mercury sat, pointedly not sweating.

Partly, this was because the Academy Administrators had deigned to turn on the air-conditioning earlier in the day, in recognition of the fact that the hall would be packed out with approximately six hundred bodies, all here to celebrate the graduation of about a third of that crowd.

But mostly, Mercury was pointedly not sweating because she made it a point never to sweat, sweat being an indication that she was working hard, and hard work being antithetical to her way of life.

However. If she *had* been sweating right now, it would not have been due to the uncomfortable warmth of six hundred packed bodies that even the air-conditioning system couldn't completely shift, or, in fact, from overexertion. Instead, it would have been caused by an even more unfamiliar concept in Mercury's emotional vocabulary: nervousness.

Mercury did not *get* nervous. Mercury got things *done*.

So the fact that she was sitting here, in the front row of the Great Hall, about to graduate from Evil Overlording Academy (with distinction), and was feeling *nervous*... She crumpled the black paper program in her pale fists. It made her furious, that's what it did.

Abjectly furious, that snooty-tooty Deviran with his stupid morals and his stupid I-don't-want-to-be-here and his stupid Overlords-are-empty-figureheads and his stupid face sitting ten people over, looking implacable with his deep brown skin and barely-there, precision-groomed beard, as though he knew it gave him a stupid air of alluringly stupid mystery…

Mercury scowled and searched for the train of thought that had been derailed, yet again, by Deviran's stupidity.

Ah. Yes. She was angry because she was nervous because she wasn't absolutely entirely one hundred and fifty percent sure that she'd beaten Deviran in their final exams, and 1) being anything less than a hundred and fifty percent certain of anything made her cranky, and 2) being beaten by Deviran for dux of the year would be utterly unbearable. She flicked away a piece of fluff that had become snagged under her immaculately magenta-painted nails and smoothed out the black paper program.

In the front corner of the hall, the starkly-attired string quartet with their traditional black instruments began playing the March of the Oncoming Doom. The screechy scrapes of hundreds of chairs on the hall's wooden floor sounded as the crowd climbed to its collective feet.

Mercury sat with her arms firmly folded for a few moments longer, until her best friend Sparky kicked her in the ankle.

"Get up, idiot," Sparky hissed, hints of real flame flickering through her flame-coloured pixie cut.

"No," Mercury said, flouncing to her feet and tossing her own glossy brown hair back over her shoulders. Four years she'd been playing by the Academy's rules in order to get what she wanted, and she'd had just about enough. Other people's rules should only be applied to plebs too stupid to invent their own.

Sparky rolled her eyes somewhere over Mercury's head before focusing on the stage, where the ceremonial party had begun entering.

Mercury clenched her jaw and narrowed her own eyes as the teachers of the Evil Overlording Academy filed onto the stage, dressed in their formal finery. Each teacher had their own distinctive look that matched their personality and their Overlording style, from severe charcoal suits to jet-black leathers, pastel ball-gowns and gem-toned lingerie and eye-blinding spandex, and even on one tiny old woman at the back, worn jeans and a grey flannel shirt. She was the one to watch out for, of course; Mercury could respect an Overlord who was confident enough in their abilities that they didn't need to telegraph them. It wasn't a look *she* would consider, of course, but still. She could respect it.

The band's march finished and, after a moderately awkward pause, the crowd sat. The Principal, pale skin and dark hair matching his suspiciously vampiric red-and-black suit, took the podium, and Mercury narrowed her eyes. He was doing a superb job of hiding his emotions—he was a premier Evil Overlord, after all—but she was Mercury, and unlike anyone else, she had the benefit of being able to rummage through people's consciousnesses. She was better at adding things *into* people's minds than taking information out, but he was telegraphing fear loudly enough that she could sense it without trying overly much.

Mercury pursed her lips.

Hmm.

The Principal cleared his throat at the blackened-wood podium, and the fear made it into his usually-unreadable eyes. "Before we begin," he said, and Mercury's stomach did a peculiar kind of flip-flop. "I have a pressing announcement to make regarding the safety of our students and their families."

He cleared his throat again and took out a sheet of paper from his pocket, unfolding it carefully and smoothing out the creases before beginning again. "The Council"—quiet booing echoed around the hall, and Mercury tsked impatiently—"have asked me to recommend that students from Tumul Tuos seriously consider postponing their return to town for a few days. The city is dealing with a *situation* at present which may present a danger to our students' health and safety."

Mercury's hands fisted at her sides and she forced herself to remain seated. What was wrong with her city? What had the Council mucked up now? A risk to the students' safety? There had to be more he wasn't telling them. Gently, Mercury tugged on his consciousness, implanting the suggestion that it might be better to share the news than to keep it secret. After all, how could they fight an enemy they didn't know?

"There are, ah…" He trailed off, glancing side to side as though wondering why his mouth had decided to continue.

Mercury didn't snicker, but she did press her lips together in satisfaction.

The Principal took a deep, steadying breath and seemed to change tack. "There has been one death already. The family have already been notified, so it is with much regret that I must inform you that Woovermyer will no longer be with us at the Evil Overlording Academy."

Murmurs broke out around the room, not all of them sad—to be expected in a school devoted to raising the next generation of dictators (ish) and despots (of sorts).

Mercury, however, crushed her program in her left hand, fist so tight her nails bit her palm.

"You okay?" Sparky murmured, leaning towards her.

Mercury gave a single, tense shake of her head and stared at the podium. Dead. Livie Woovermyer was dead in *her city*. And the Council hadn't done anything to stop it. Couldn't do anything to stop it, probably, given they'd warned the students to stay away. Livie hadn't been the strongest candidate in the year level, but she was no lightweight, either. It would take a lot of power to kill a Seven.

Enough was enough. A good thing Mercury was about to graduate at the top of the class, giving her the right to knock the lowest ranking current Overlord off their perch. Tumul Tuos would be hers in a matter of hours. And then there'd be no more of these wasteful deaths. Her city would be safe at last.

Madame Pompadour was up the front now, elbow gloves the same glimmery silver colour as her elaborate, piled-curls wig, eyelids gleaming with matching silver eye shadow, and abruptly Mercury realised Madame was there to make the announcement that would change her life forever. She leaned forward in her seat, ready to stand when her name was called.

"And now the announcement you've all been dying for," the Political Alliances teacher trilled, the frills on her evening gown fluttering as she moved. "The dux of this year's cohort!"

Sweat slicked Mercury's palms. Irritated, she reached over and wiped them on Sparky's thigh.

Sparky pushed Mercury's hands back into her own personal space bubble and Mercury, nervous to the edge of distraction, let her.

"Will you please join me in welcoming to the stage, our wonderful dux for this year, Deviran Goodsmith!"

Mercury froze halfway to standing. "Did she just say Deviran?" she whispered furiously to Sparky.

Sparky hauled her forcibly back down into her seat. "Yes," she hissed back. "Sit down, you're making a fool of yourself."

Mercury's spine snapped upright as she sat, and she arranged the folds of her long black skirt demurely. "No I'm not." She closed her eyes. "Deviran's going up to the stage, isn't he?" Even at a whisper, the misery in her voice was clear, but this time, she didn't care.

Sparky reached over and squeezed her hand.

Mercury squeezed back, lacing her fingers through Sparky's, and held tight as all her plans and dreams vanished in front of her.

A stone had landed in her chest. That must be it. Some strange sort of magic that made her chest contract and sink, and made the world distort for just a moment, long enough to trick her into thinking Deviran had beaten her so that someone could jump in front of her and yell SURPRISE!

Any moment now.

Any moment.

She refused to open her eyes and watch Deviran parading across the stupid stage like some stupid stupid-person, receiving his stupid medal and stupid symbolic crest pin.

It was that last exam question. She'd known Deviran would pull out his ridiculous 'Evil Overlords are merely figureheads, the Business Guild is where the power really lies' rant that everyone had heard a million times back when he was younger and angrier, and she'd tried to counter it, she really had.

She'd argued for the importance of the Overlording position, for the power of having a symbolic figure to unite the population in their hatred, for having a person able to make all the difficult, necessary decisions the Council was too weak and spineless to make... But it hadn't been enough. Everything she'd worked for, everything she'd set out to prove—and it wasn't enough.

There were words, there were names, and then forever later, once she'd died twice already, Sparky elbowed her in the ribs. "Come on," Sparky muttered. "We're up next."

And sure enough, there was a shuffling of presenters as the last of the Powers Behind The Thone graduates departed the stage, and the next speaker announced in threatening, funereal tones, "The Overlording cohort."

Mercury blinked furiously and followed Sparky to the end of the line at the right side of the stage. The other candidates proceeded one at a time across the stage, two girls and then stupid Deviran, and then a handful more and then Sparky, and then the speaker was calling her name.

Hands fisted, Mercury tossed her head high, climbed the four steps, and marched across the stage. She wouldn't look at them, the stupid faculty who'd denied her the city she rightfully deserved, and she wouldn't look the other way either, at the classmates and crowd undoubtedly sniggering at her failure.

She shook hands with the presenter, and while he pinned the tiny crossedswords badge on her collar, her eyes betrayed her and slid towards the audience. Her stomach flipped as she saw the crowd of parents and friends behind the rows of students, all the way to the back of the hall, twenty rows at least, illuminated by the late afternoon light streaming in through the ceiling-high windows to the right. Everyone had someone here to watch them graduate. Everyone except Weird Al—and her.

The presenter finished with her pin, muttered something to her, and offered his hand again. Mercury coldly ignored it and strode from the stage. It didn't matter. None of it mattered. Tumul Tuos was her city anyway, and no one could change that. She'd think of something. She'd take a day or two out, make some plans...

And she could always hope that Deviran would choose some other Overlording territory. He'd be stupid to, but then again, he was stupid, so. Mercury could hope.

All at once, mid-way down the steps off the stage, Mercury came to rigid attention, scanning the room. Somewhere out there in the crowd, an exchange of power had just taken place, and it felt... unusual.

But the final few students were backing up behind her and muttering, so Mercury headed back toward her seat, craning her head all the while and searching for some sign of whatever it was that had just discharged a dizzyingly quiet amount of power into the room.

She sat, and Sparky leaned over. "Okay?"

"Mm," said Mercury. "Did you feel…" She accidentally caught the eye of the student behind her and twisted back to face the front.

"Feel what?"

Mercury turned it over in her mind. It had felt like a large shot of power discharged very quietly—but perhaps it hadn't been. Perhaps it had only been a small discharge after all, something most people wouldn't have noticed.

But still, something about it had tugged on her. It very nearly felt like something she'd felt before, only she *knew* she'd never sensed that kind of discharge before.

She shook her head. "Never mind. Don't worry."

Sparky sighed and straightened. "It's fine, Mercury," she said, drily exasperated.

"I know you didn't win, but I promise, you'll live through it."

Mercury waved a hand for silence.

The power had just discharged again, and it had come from somewhere in the back corner, far away from the windows and light.

Impatiently, Mercury waited for the formalities to conclude. The crowd stood while the quartet played the exit march, and the stage party left, Mercury tapping her foot all the while.

The moment the last notes of the march died away, Mercury turned and headed to the back corner, weaving in and out of the students and parents who had seemed to explode slowly but inexorably out from the neat rows of seating, ignoring Sparky's calls behind her. Power, something that tugged in a way that was strange and familiar, all at once. She pushed her way through a family posing for pictures—and halted.

In the shadows of the back corner, Deviran stood with his family, with his stupid, smug little smile, looking as tall and dark and stupidly alluring as ever. Prat.

His mother, short but sleek, and his father—tall, and utterly terrifying in a way not at all diminished by his gleaming smile—gushed over him, patting his back and hugging him tight. Within moments the Principal was there, glibly shaking hands and congratulating them on the success of their son. Something flickered across his consciousness, and also Deviran's father's—some moment of recognition in response to what they were saying.

But Mercury brushed it aside just as the mother brushed melodramatic tears from her cheeks and handed Deviran a silver-wrapped package about as long as her hand but half the width.

That. That was the source of the strange, magical feeling. Mercury watched hawk-eyed as Deviran un-wrapped the gift. A glimpse of gold set her pulse racing—What was it? What did it do? Could she steal it?—and then the paper fell away to the floor, and Deviran stood staring wordlessly at the object in his hands, and Mercury did too.

Wide-eyed, Deviran raised his gaze to his parents, and even from where she stood Mercury could hear the reverence in his voice as he thanked them.

But Mercury had eyes only for the object. No wonder she'd felt it discharge, and no wonder it had felt both strange and familiar. In Deviran's hands lay a glorious, sunshine-gold key, large and strong—and with a handle in the shape of a stylised fish, long, flowing fins curving to make the grip.

A Key. They'd given him a Key. And not just any Key, but *the* Key, *her* Key, the Artefact of Power belonging to *her* city.

A wordless noise of wanting rose in Mercury's throat. Who cared about being dux? She needed that Key.

Keep reading! Head to
www.amylaurens.com/books/
kaditeos/castle
to buy your copy now!

ABOUT THE AUTHOR

AMY LAURENS is an Australian author of fantasy fiction for all ages. She doesn't usually wear a lot of make-up, to be honest, but she does appreciate some killer eyeliner when the situation calls for it.

In addition to moderately twisted little stories, Amy has also written the award-winning fantasy *Sanctuary* series about Edge, a 13-year-old girl forced to move to a small country town because of witness protection (the first book is *Where Shadows Rise*), the humorous fantasy *Kaditeos* series, following newly graduated Evil Overlord Mercury as she attempts to acquire a castle, the forthcoming young adult *Storm Foxes* series about magic and mental health, and a whole host of non-fiction.

INKLETS

Collect them all! Released on the 1st and 15th of each month.

Welcome to Dark Dale
LIANA BROOKS

When War Came to Town
A Powers Story
AMY LAURENS

Not Fantasy
AMY LAURENS

Courting the Winter Prince
LIANA BROOKS

At the Home of the Winter King
A Storm Foster Story
AMY LAURENS

With This Ring
AMY LAURENS

Venus &
Seven Reasons I Said No
LIANA BROOKS

OATH KEEPER
AMY LAURENS

FORGET
A Powers Story
AMY LAURENS

INKLET #040
Not quite
Cinderella
LIANA BROOKS

INKLET #041
ONE BAD MAN
AMY LAURENS

DOUBLE ISSUE!
INKLET #042
The Claustrophobia
Of Loneliness &
Adam, Be A Star
AMY LAURENS

INKLET #043
The Artist
as a Young Girl
LIANA BROOKS

INKLET #044
CONFESSIONS
AMY LAURENS

INKLET #045
But For Snow
A Kaitics Story
AMY LAURENS

INKLET #046
The Boy
Named NO
LIANA BROOKS

INKLET #047
Anamata
AMY LAURENS

INKLET #048
A Wolf for
Christmas
AMY LAURENS